# ACKNOWLEDGEMENTS

Cover illustrated by Asur.
Find more of their art here:
www.artstation.com/asur-misoa


To Josh for hosting the sessions in which
these characters were incepted.


To Dani and Arte who listened and laughed
when we read them our drafts.

# CONTENTS

# PART ONE, THE START OF A... BEAUTIFUL FRIENDSHIP

"That one down there?" asked a bandit.

"What do you think boss?"

"He's all alone, five against one." Darkcloak responded.

"But boss, there's six of us."

"Not against him there isn't, there's five of you."

"He's pretty big though…"

"I have complete faith in your abilities. I'll be right behind you. Not right, right behind you. But a safe distance right behind you."

The bandits moved down through the trees. They cowered behind branches and held their breath. One and two, the orc moved down the path. Left foot then right. A breath and a grunt. The men signed to each other, you first, signed one. No you, replied the other. The orc stopped, he looked around and breathed in heavily.

"I smell injustice."

"Attack!" shouted Darkcloak. The men screamed, running from their hiding spots toward the orc. The first to charge the orc found his face against a shield, whilst the second found the axe. The third man tried to grab on, but was pushed to the floor. The orc bellowed, hit out with his shield and then swung his axe cutting through his attackers. Only one remained. The man tried to run, but slipped over a friend's corpse. The orc grabbed on by the leg and swung the attacker through the air. The force ripped body from leg, leaving the orc with an axe in one hand and a leg in the other.

Darkcloak watched, his mouth agape. "Oh," he said. Purcee grunted.

"You saved me! Yes. From those bandits. Of whom I was not affiliated with. Those ones."

"Bandit keep you prisoner?"

"Um… yes. Yes, they did. They'd been forcing me to work as their guide through this forest, you see. That's why I was here with them. Yes." Darkcloak knelt to loot the corpses of his fallen brethren.

"Tyr smite thieves." The orc dropped the leg.

"Oh, I'm not a thief, noble… noble orc. This gold was mine, you see. These bandits stole it from me."

"They thief?"

"Yes."

"But you not thief?"

"No."

"I agree."

"You do? Yes, you do! Good! You're a very clever… person. I'm Darkcloak… but that sounds like a bandit name so I'm actually… Barry. Yes Barry Darkcloak, Mr Barry Darkcloak."

"Purcee." The orc hit his chestplate.

"You're Purcee? That's your name?"

"Purcee."

"You're a paladin, right?"

"Tyr my god."

"The god of... what's he the god of again?"

"Justice."

"Justice, yes! Now I remember. Good old Tear. He's one of my favourites."

"Tyr."

"That's what I said."

"No."

"You probably just misheard me, my scary new friend. We're in a forest, after all. I don't need to tell you about... forest acoustics. But I needn't fear cause I'm just. Very just. Back home they used to call me Barry the Just. Because of how just I was. And still continue to be."

"Back home me small giant."

"That's what they called you, you mean? Was that because you're giant, but not as giant as the giant... giants?" Purcee began to leave. "Where are you headed to, Purcee the small giant?"

"Purcee hate small giant."

"You do?"

"Make Purcee feel giant yet small."

"Okay then, Purcee, Paladin of Tyr, most just of us all... Where you heading?"

"To justice."

"Uh-huh. Well, what a coincidence! You see, before I was kidnapped by those fearsome bandits, who I had no prior connections to and wasn't in league with at all, I was busy investigating a particularly unjust merchant in the next town over. Perhaps you'd like to help me... bring him to justice?"

"Tyr will smite!"

"A smite, huh? Well, I was thinking we could just rob him... of his ill gotten gains, that is."

"Purcee pray." Purcee knelt down to pray.

"What's the timescale for a response from the almighty?"

Purcee grunted in response.

"Will he get back to you quite quick?"

Purcee didn't respond.

"Well, you should probably get to it, then. I'll just, uh... stand over here."

Purcee dug his shield into the ground and then placed his axe in between. As he began to pray the axe started to glow. "Close eyes." Purcee spoke. Barry turned his back and closed his eyes. He cupped his hands to his face. He could not see the light, but he could hear it hum. He could feel it as it brushed against his skin, he felt the very air around him part momentarily as the light passed through the trees.

"Merchant unjust."

"He is? I mean, uh... yes, he is. That's why we should rob him."

"Smite him."

"Smiting is also good, yes. And then can we rob him?"

"No."

"No. Of course not. No robbing. Certainly not. Yes."

# PART TWO, THE MERCHANT THAT WAS A MEAN AND NOT VERY NICE PERSON

"Tell me." Purcee asked.

"What about?" said Barry.

"Merchant."

"Well, his name is Glenn Kirkup. He's a merchant. And he's... unjust? He charges exorbitant prices, and he always looked down on me, that too."

"Where be?"

"I would say..." Barry looked around, "in there." He pointed over to a building.

"Inn?"

"Yes."

"No."

"No?"

"Yes."

"I think it's worth an investigation," said Barry, heading towards the inn.

"No, human."

"I'm not a human, I'm a halfling. And I'm quite tall

for a halfling, I'll have you know. Now come on."

The pair headed inside, attracting the gaze of many onlookers. The music ceased for a second, before curious minds became calm and moved back to their drinks. Three gnomes went back to the piano; it took all of them to play it at full range.

Barry headed to the bar, dragging a chair over to stand on. "Barkeep!"

"You…" The barkeep looked at Barry. ""What do you want, Darkcloak?"

"Just a drink and information."

"Why should I give you either? You didn't pay last time, and I don't care for conversation."

"Well, you see my friend over there? He's here to settle my debts."

"Which friend would that be, huh?"

"Big and scary over there."

"The Paladin!"

"The one and only."

"The Paladin's yer friend?"

"Yes."

"Who's he devoted to, the God of Swindlers?"

"Nope, to Tyr."

"What! You brought a devotee of Tyr here. Are you suicidal? You trying to get us all killed?"

"Well, that depends."

"On what?"

"On if you put our drinks on the tab, and then throw out the tab."

"I'll tell Glenn about all this, see what he thinks." The barkeeper hissed to Barry as Purcee walked over.

"Glenn?" Purcee asked resting his axe against the bar.

"No, I'm the barkeep. Glenn's a merchant in these parts."

"Him bad."

"He has a good side too, probably, when he isn't leading that guild of death of his."

"A death guild?" Barry asked.

"Glenn sounds like a mean and not very nice person," said Purcee.

"I don't think I've heard you say a sentence that long. Well done, my large orc friend."

"Smite."

"And how are we going to do that exactly?"

"Smite him."

"But he has guards and if you kill him in his shop we won't have any proof of his wrongdoings."

"I heard that there is a meeting to discuss guild business tonight in the cemetery," the barkeeper chimed in.

"I smite him."

"You mean in the meeting that every thief and murderer will be attending?"

"Yes."

"Well, sure, that seems sensible!"

"Tyr guides me." Purcee picked up his axe and left.

"Well, Darkcloak, it has been a genuine displeasure knowing you, and I hope Glenn ends you both slowly," the barkeep sneered.

"And I hope the people in here don't find out you water down the drinks." Barry followed Purcee out.

The inn was now quiet, the patrons stared at the bar-keeper.

# PART THREE, A CONFRONTATION OF SORTS

"So, uh… Purcee?"

"Barry?"

"How's this for an idea: instead of walking into a group full of murderers in a dark cemetery at night time, why don't we just head to Glenn's shop, knowing he won't be there, and rob the place?"

"No rob, only smite." The paladin was walking at full stride towards the cemetery, with Barry struggling to keep up.

"But, uh, Purcee, do you maybe think this might be… dangerous? I mean, I get you're a big guy and I know you can handle yourself in a fight. I mean, the way you took out my band of thieves - I mean, uh… that band of thieves that had taken me prisoner… You swatted them like flies, but I think…" Barry stopped and scratched his head. "Actually, what am I saying? These guys aren't even going to scratch you, are they?"

"No."

"A cemetery full of thieves… that's going to be a lot of gold… Onwards, for justice!"

"Justice!"

"Also, the cemetery is this way." Barry pointed back the way they'd been walking.

Purcee turned around. "Justice," he whispered.

\*\*\*

When the pair arrived at the cemetery, the sun had almost set, the sky as red as a Crystopian apple. Through the gravestones came a dozen voices, chanting in unison. Glenn Kirkup and his followers, clad in dark robes, looked less like a band of criminals and more like a demonic cult.

*Oh great one, Bhaal, god of death, god of murder and theft. Taketh my blood, and give me gold taketh from the pockets of unknowing victims to your slaughter. Bhaal blessed be, besiege us with knowledge, breathe onto us your rage, extrude us of our compassion. Let us be animals, let us forget mercy, allow us to profit from your wisdom. We loyally serve thee, and we do beseech to you two sacrifices.*

"I don't see any sacrifices," Barry whispered.

Purcee grunted. His grunt carried on the wind.

Glenn stared at Purcee and Barry. *Oh great one, thou hast brought the small giant and giant small.*

"I'm a halfling!" Barry snipped. "And he doesn't like being called a small giant, it makes him feel giant, yet small."

"Smite!"

*You would smite me for worshipping Bhaal?*

"Yes."

*Surround them disciples. Rob them of their weapons, cut into their flesh, string them up so we may bleed them for the ceremony.*

"Erm, Purcee? I don't like the sound of that."

"No."

"No, it all sounds rather unpleasant. Particularly the bit about the cutting, the stringing, and the bleeding. All the parts, really."

"Tyr will smite!"

"Just knock the hat off Glenn's smug face. And then knock his face off too."

Barry covered his eyes. He heard the hum first, he could feel it radiate around him. The dirt around Purcee began to lift, then the stones too. The trees around the cemetery bent inwards from the top. The sky exploded a bolt of concentrated light which flooded into Purcee's axe. Everything held still for a moment, the dirt and stones floated around Purcee in a vortex, the trees reached inwards like a crab. Glenn looked at Purcee and tried to swear Bhaal away, but it was too late. His past crimes would not be forgiven, this was Tyr's will.

"Justice!" Purcee screamed as the light exploded from his axe, multitudes brighter and more powerful. The dirt and stones flew out impacting the cultists. The trees snapped backwards uprooting them, the light blinded all that saw it, it scorched the flesh of the cultists, breaking through to bones that shattered by the very force. When the light subsided Barry opened his eyes. He had been left alone by Tyr's wrath. He looked around, where once there was cultists now there was ash. The trees had fallen, scorched by the divine light. Steam raised from Purcee's armour. It was red hot, but the orc seemed unaffected. Purcee fell to the floor.

"Are you okay?" Barry asked.

"Smite tiring," Purcee responded before he passed out.

"Hah, 'Tyr'ing. I get it. Uh… Purcee?" Barry prodded the paladin with his foot. "Well," he said, looking around at the carnage. "It's a good thing I'm a good guy. Yup."

Barry looked over to where Glenn had stood, half in disbelief. "That isn't possible." Barry exclaimed. Glenn was on the floor, still breathing. He hadn't turned to ashes.

*Bhaal protected me. The hat of Bhaal saved me from divine punishment.*

"The hat of Bhaal, huh? What happens if I take it off?"

*What?*

Barry removed the hat. Nothing seemed to happen.

You cannot best the God of Death.

"That seemed anticlimactic," said Barry. He reached for his dagger, but before he could grab it Glenn started screaming. His flesh began to melt, his bones crumbled, he dispersed into ash and joined his god. The sacrifices had been made, just not the ones Glenn had hoped for. All that remained was his hat.

"Hmm," Barry thought, "this is a nice hat…"

# PART FOUR, DRINKS ARE ON ME

"Purcee, wake up." Barry nudged Purcee. "It's morning, Purcee, I need you to wake up. Power like yours is something I very much like having on my side."

Purcee began to mumble.

"Purcee, what are you trying to say? Speak up." Barry leant in to try to catch Purcee's words.

"Hungry, so hungry."

"I guess smiting takes a lot out of an orc."

"Need food."

"Well, the nearest place would be the inn, if you like spit in your food."

"No."

"Well maybe more my food than yours."

"Yes."

***

Purcee and Barry hobbled into the inn. The barkeeper's jaw dropped. "Darkcloak! But... you two should be dead!"

"Well, sorry to disappoint you."

"You should at least be hurt."

"Hungry," Purcee interjected.

Barry pulled a chair up to the counter, climbing up and grabbing the barkeeper by the neck. "You set us up, you smarmy swineherd. Now, if you want to remain unharmed, I suggest you... get us some food."

"What? You just want... food?"

"Yup." Barry let go of the barkeeper and, climbing down, made his way over to a table. "On the house, of course."

"No spit," added Purcee as he sat down at the table.

"What's next?" Barry asked, half afraid of the answer.

"Purcee pray."

"Is that your response to every situation? I mean, I guess it's worked so far..."

Purcee knelt down to pray. The food arrived, Barry ate, Purcee's food went cold. Purcee stood up.

"You prayed for a while."

"Tyr quiet, something wrong."

"Well, he did just help you smite a mob of cultists. Maybe he is having a nap too."

"Tyr never nap."

"What does this mean, then?"

"We go, Crystopia. To temple. Bhaal corrupt temple. Block Tyr."

"Then we will just have to go there and smite them, right?"

"Without Tyr, no smite."

"You mean... but, how do we beat the cultists?"

"We fight."

"I'm worried that it won't be a fair fight."

"Then we die."

"Is there a third option?"

"No."

"So… that's a no, then?"

"No."

"Okay then. Will you carry me there?"

"No."

# PART FIVE, A CHAMPION NAMED COLIN

"This journey would have been easier if you'd carried me."

"No."

"Well, anyway, here we are in chrysalis. Or whatever it's called. Christopher. Cartographer."

"Crystopia."

"That is definitely what I said, but never mind. Let's find an inn, shall we?"

"Temple."

"But a drink to calm our nerves."

"Temple."

"The one thing I hate about temples is their lack of alcohol, and their murder cults, when they have them. But generally the lack of alcohol. Murder cults aren't so bad when you're drunk."

"No drink." Purcee lead the way to the temple. They reached the thousand steps.

"How many steps?"

"Many."

"But..."

"We climb."

"Can you carry me?"

"No."

"Well then, maybe I'll just stay here... Have fun in the evil temple." Purcee grabbed Barry by the scruff of his neck and dropped him on the first step. They started climbing, Purcee, being a small giant, went up the steps with ease; however with Barry being a giant small it meant he was climbing and clambering up each step.

"I feel we've been climbing for hours. I'm exhausted! How many steps have we done?"

"Twelve."

"It has to be more than that."

"Twelve."

"How many more?"

"Eighty-Two more..."

"Eighty-Two more?"

"Eighty-Two more, lots of twelve."

"This is how I die."

"Barry, follow."

***

When they reached the top they found the temple's large wooden doors were shut.

"Well, that's a shame, the temple seems to be closed, looks like we'll have to come back another day."

Purcee grunted.

"At least all those cultists don't know we're here."

Purcee knocked on the door.

"What are you doing? The cultists will hear you."

Purcee knocked louder.

"Stop it." Barry pulled Purcee's arm. "The door isn't going to open."

"Open." Purcee spoke, "Open." He declared. "OPEN!"

"Are you trying to intimidate the door?"

"Open door," Purcee intimidated.

"You can't intimidate a door, Purcee. It's made of wood. It's inanimate. It's not just going to open…" The door clunked and opened inward. "That was just a coincidence!"

"Door intimidated."

A monk poked his head around the door. "Oi!" said the monk. "Stop scaring my door!"

Purcee grunted, startling the monk. "Aah!" said the monk.

A second, older monk poked his head around the door. "Oi!" said the second monk. "Stop scaring my novice!"

Barry stepped in front of Purcee. "Greetings, humble monks!"

"We ain't humble!" barked the first monk. "We're actually quite smug."

"And proud of it!" said the second monk, nodding in agreement.

"Have you, erm, checked the temple for cultists of Bhaal?" Barry asked.

"That seems oddly specific," answered one of the monks.

"We check for cultists and florists every fortnight," responded the other.

"And when was the last time you checked?" Barry asked.

"Umm… thirteen days ago."

"So… can we check the temple?"

"No, not until tomorrow."

Purcee stepped forward, his large frame squeezing into the slightly smaller frame of the door. "Now."

The two monks stepped back. "Well, uh, maybe we could check a day early… But let me tell you, this will throw our whole schedule right off." Purcee pushed past them and headed towards the temple sanctum. He pushed open the doors to see an interior desecrated by Bhaal's worshippers. There were bodies hanging from the ceiling by their own entrails. In the center of the room the statue to Tyr had been sullied, it was smeared in blood and now adorned with a hat of Bhaal which blocked Tyr's presence in the realm.

"Oh my goodness, what happened here? Look at this! There's been… There's been cultists all up in our temple. When could they have done this?" exclaimed the novice monk.

"I don't know, but this must have happened after the last check, so at most twelve days ago."

"How could this have happened under our watch? How could we not have noticed all these cultists running around? Cultists who are certainly not here any more, as you can plainly see."

Purcee grunted. Barry moved his hand to the dagger on his belt. "Uh-huh… Plainly."

"Well, I suppose you two should be going. The cultists have clearly fled, probably because they heard you were coming, so well done! We'll stay and clean up this mess."

"Are you two the cultists?" said Barry.

"Whaaat?" said the first monk. "That is... that is completely absurd." He turned to the second monk. "Isn't that absurd?"

"I think the game's up." The monks drew razor sharp daggers from their robes. "You two just had to poke around, didn't you?" Said the second monk. "Well, now I guess we'll be doing some poking around... In your guts! With our knives!"

"Yeah!" said the first monk. "We're gonna stab you!"

"Yeah, I got that," said Barry, drawing his own knife. "It wasn't lost on me at all."

Purcee stepped in front of Barry, raising his axe. "Smite."

The monks wavered. "Colin! Help!"

"Who's Colin?" Barry asked.

"The muscle."

"I should have figured there'd be more of you monks."

"Colin isn't a monk, he's our champion."

Colin walked into the room. He was an orc, but bigger than Purcee. He wore spiked armor and a hat of Bhaal. He wielded a warhammer and his eyes were as dark as death.

"Blessed be Bhaal!" he spoke.

"Blessed be Tyr," Purcee shouted.

"You sacrifice!" Colin declared.

"Smite!" yelled Purcee as he ran towards Colin.

"Smash!" yelled Colin as he ran to meet Purcee.

The two orcs met with an almighty clash, striking blows that would have instantly killed any human, or halfling, or gnome, or elf; be it high elf, wood elf, dark elf, sea elf, festive winter elf, or even the exceedingly rare and optimistic lava elf. Although, come to think of it a stone elf might have survived, but certainly no other type of elf.

Barry and the two monks stood off to the side, a little awkwardly.

"This is usually over by now," said the first monk.

"Uh-huh." said Barry.

"We, uh… we don't usually do the fighting ourselves. I hope you don't mind," said the second monk.

"No, that's okay," said Barry.

"I'm Terry by the way, and that's Mort."

"I'm Barry, that's Purcee."

"We don't really get to socialise much."

"That's probably because we're part of a murder cult and we kill everyone we meet. Your friend is really scary by the way."

"I'll let you guys in on a little secret, he isn't my friend at all; I barely know him. I tried to rob him, but accidentally became his travelling companion. The guy might as well spit out gold the amount of people he kills. I've just been picking up the crumbs."

"Well, that changes things."

"It does?"

"We thought you'd fight to the death next to your orc, but if you're as awful a person as you've said, there might just be a position for you in the armies of Bhaal."

"I could definitely see you filling one of the hats." responded the other.

"I actually have one," Barry mentioned, pulling it out

and resting it on his head.

"Oh my, yes. That looks wonderful."

"Truly a sight."

"You really think so?"

"Definitely."

Barry looked over at Purcee, who seemed to be getting the upper hand. He was punching Colin in the face whilst repeating the words "Tyr, Tyr, Tyr, Tyr…"

"As much as I'd love to join you guys in your fun little death cult of gruesome carnage, murder really isn't my thing, and I think we can both see which is the winning team here. So I'm going to have to decline your offer, but I do thank you for the opportunity." Barry flipped his knife in his hand, "Now, before Purcee finishes up, you two should really surrender - your weapons and your purses."

Colin's eye was now bloodshot from Purcee's fists. Purcee went to punch again, but Colin ducked and Purcee's fist impacted against the solid marble floor. Purcee screamed as Colin tackled him. He tried to get out of Colin's grasp but couldn't, he took a knee to the chest and was pushed into the door. Colin grabbed Purcee's head and pulled it back before slamming it into the wood. He pulled it back once again, and then hit it back against the door, splintering it. Colin grabbed Purcee by the armour and dragged him. Purcee tried to resist but he was kicked down to the ground at the top of the thousand steps.

"Tyr weak, Bhaal strong." Colin declared.

"No." Purcee mumbled.

"Tyr weak, Bhaal strong." the orc repeated.

"No!" Purcee shouted through bloodied lips. "Tyr true." Purcee pushed himself to his feet.

"Tyr weak. You weak too." Colin kicked Purcee, sending him tumbling down the steps.

Barry looked over at Colin, and then back at the grinning monks. "So, your cult. How are the hours? Is the pay good?"

"Too late, shorty." The monks pointed their daggers at Barry. Colin, having

finished with Purcee, came lumbering over, a wicked smile on his face. "Smaaash…"

"Uh, um, you saved me!" Barry squeaked. The orc stopped, confused.

"Saved… you?"

"Yeah, of course! You saved me from that paladin! Well done, you!"

Mort rolled his eyes. "Please, do you really think that's going to work?"

"Look!" said Barry, pointing to his hat of Bhaal. "Look! I've got a hat! Like yours! These guys don't have hats, see? That means they're not with us!"

"Hmm… Smaaash… them?" said Colin, glaring at the hatless monks.

"Yes. You do that."

"Smash!" Colin ran past Barry and lashed out at Mort and Terry. He swung the warhammer which fractured Terry's skull on impact. Colin then swung the warhammer round again to hit the other monk. Mort was sprier than Terry had been and ducked out of the way. Colin came round for another swing, missing Mort again but hitting the statue with such force that it toppled.

Barry started to back out of the room.

Mort dodged another swing and countered, stabbing upwards into Colin's throat.

Barry continued towards the door.

Colin grunted at his wound but it didn't slow him, he pushed forward until he had Mort cornered. Colin lifted his warhammer for a final blow.

Barry had reached the door by now and peered back out of morbid curiosity.

Mort stabbed Colin again in the chest but the hammer had too much power behind it, there was nothing that could stop it crushing Mort's ribs in on themselves, puncturing his lungs and stopping his heart. Colin touched his throat and grunted. He fell to the floor beside Mort.

Barry edged into the doorway. "I think that went well. I think that went quite well, all things considered. I think that went... yes." Barry walked out the door, leaving the two dead monks and Colin behind.

# PART SIX, REST A BIT, WORRY A BIT MORE

Purcee woke up in a bed many sizes too small for him. His armour had been removed. The blankets weren't big enough to cover all of his body. His skin was a mosaic of scars and bruises, like a canvas that had been scratched by a brush too coarse. "Purcee," he whimpered. He stood but didn't realise how low the ceiling was and knocked his head. "Purcee." He whimpered again. The door to the room opened and the handle hit him in the leg. "Purcee hurt." He whined.

"I am so sorry." A clean cut man dressed in pristine silver armour with a white cloak stepped through the doorway. "This is the biggest room we had free. I couldn't just leave a big guy like you to die on the street."

"Purcee find Barry."

"Is Barry your friend?"

"Find Barry."

"Listen there, my name's Ted. I'm a city guardsman. Well, I'm the captain of the guard now, that's going to take some getting used to."

"Guard Captain, help Barry."

"Help, how?"

"Cult temple."

"Oh, the worshippers of Bhaal are no longer a problem," spoke a second guard who had stepped into the room. She had red hair that flowed onto her shoulders from beneath her helmet. "Their bodies are being cleared out as we speak."

"Was body halfling?" Purcee asked.

"What?"

"Bodies, is there halfling?"

"No halflings."

"Barry alive."

"You want to tell us what happened in there?" the captain asked.

"No."

"Did you defeat the cultists?" the guard asked.

"No."

"But you were there?" she continued.

"Yes."

The captain waved his hand, dismissively. "Clarisse, stop interrogating our new friend. Whatever went on at that old temple doesn't matter anymore. What's important - Purcee, was it? - is that we get you back in fighting form as soon as possible. I think you'll be a great help to us."

"Help you?"

"Yes, indeed. You're a paladin, no? You can help us keep the peace in this great city. It will be well worth your efforts, I assure you."

"Justice...?"

"Yes, that's right! I think you and I will get on just fine." The Captain smiled, turning on his heels to leave. "You rest a while longer, small giant. We'll see you in the morning." And he was gone. The other guard, Clarisse, stayed.

"You should be careful in this city, paladin," she said. "Not everything is what it seems."

"Purcee strong."

"And how did that work out for you at the temple? Like the captain said, you should rest longer. I'll look out for your friend." And with that, she was gone too, leaving Purcee alone. He sat back down on the bed, the frame barely supporting his weight.

"Purcee." He said. He went to pray but as he closed his eyes to find Tyr, sleep found him.

# PART SEVEN, THE PIOUS PALADIN

When Purcee awoke the next morning, he was already feeling much better. It seemed it was true what the guards had told him about the temple - the cultists had been purged, and Purcee's connection to Tyr was returning, helping to mend his broken body. Purcee wondered what had happened to Barry, and how his small friend had managed to fight all three cultists. He hoped the halfling was safe.

Purcee's thoughts were interrupted by a knock on the door. Without waiting for an answer, Captain Ted walked in. "Purcee! Good morning! Why, you're looking stronger than ever! I mean, I suppose the first time I saw you you were unconscious and half-dead, but that's besides the point..."

"Tyr renews me," said Purcee, solemnly.

"Uh-huh. Well, my friend, how say you we take a trip down to the market? On official business, of course! We're going to, ah... collect some tributes from the citizens there."

Purcee found his feet, being careful not to hit his head on the ceiling this time, he followed the captain out of the small room and found himself in a corridor that seemed to lead to dozens of rooms like the one he'd just left. Clarisse was waiting for them, a frown on her face.

"This is our stronghold, Purcee," the captain said, leading them down the corridor. "We'll save the tour for later. I expect for now you'll want some food."

Purcee's stomach rumbled, reminding the orc of how hungry he was. "Food good."

"Yes, indeed! The best food you've ever eaten will taste like dirt next to the stuff they sell in the market here. And for us, it's all free! You should have seen the city only a few years ago," Ted continued talking as they left the stronghold and walked towards the market. "Crime everywhere, the streets filthy with litter, no one was safe. Well, we've sorted two of those things out. Have you ever tasted a Crystopian apple, Purcee?"

"No."

"They are sweeter than the apples you'd find in the lesser city states like Brunda, and Purrell. Do you know why?"

"No."

"Because Brunda and Purrell can't grow apples like we can. Their trees wither and grow limp, whilst ours grow brazen and strong. We only sell Crystopian apples, whereas Brunda and Purrell need to have apples shipped to them. This is what makes Crystopia strong.

"Apples?"

"No, we do things for ourselves. We take what we need and we never waste anything. Like a big guy like you, you're what we need. It would be stupid if we were to waste your... gifts."

They reached the market. Ted strutted around and

grabbed an apple and threw it to Purcee. "Taste it Purcee, this is one of Crystopia's finest."

"Pay."

"As I told you, my large friend, everything here is free for us guards."

Purcee walked over to the vendor and reached into his pocket. The vender flinched backwards. Purcee withdrew some gold and dropped it into the vendors shaking palm. "Tyr blesses you."

"What are you doing, Purcee?" Ted exclaimed.

"Purcee not guard. Purcee pay."

Ted laughed, shaking his head. "Oh, Purcee. You don't have to pay, because you're with us!" He walked over to the vendor, clasping the man's shoulder with his gloved hand. "You don't expect us to pay for our apples, do you?"

"No, of course not…" said the trembling merchant.

"No, that's good, because you know we're here to protect you. It would be terrible if we couldn't protect you, wouldn't it?"

"Yes, terrible…"

"See, Purcee? We're helping these peasant- sorry, pleasant… pleasant people. We're their protectors. So, we don't pay."

"It's just as he says, large sir," stammered the merchant. "You don't need to pay me. But thank you, and may Tyr bless you."

"Anyway," Ted spoke, "we need to be collecting the protect… I mean the charity funds."

"Charity?"

"Yes, the merchants here have had a good quarter

and as such are paying ten percent of their earnings so that we may distribute it to the most needing of citizens." The vendor placed some gold into a pouch and handed it to Ted. "Here Purcee," Ted threw the pouch, "you can hold onto this, there's no chance any would-be thief would try to prey on you."

Ted and Purcee continued around the stalls collecting the 'charity' money. Some vendors were more willing to participate than others. "Greedy vendors," Ted exclaimed to Purcee between stalls, "You'd think we were asking the world of them." The pouch was now nearly overflowing.

Clarisse came over and pulled Ted over to one side. They seemed to be discussing something intently. Purcee spotted a beggar to the side of the street. He walked over. The beggar stooped his head, believing Purcee to be a guard.

"May Tyr bless you, with charity." Purcee smiled and handed over the pouch. The beggar stared down, looking in disbelief at the gold. "T-t-thank you." The beggar stuttered before making a quick exit. Purcee headed back through the stalls towards Ted and Clarisse.

"Purcee, my small giant companion. Tell Clarisse how you've been keeping the gold in safe hands for us."

"Charity."

"Yes, it will be going to 'charity' yes, all of it."

"It with charity."

"...What?"

"Tyr bless you."

Ted looked at Clarisse who tilted her head to the side and lifted her brow whilst smiling.

"Tyr blesses us all I see," Ted spoke through his teeth.

# PART EIGHT, A ROGUISH REUNION

Barry was in the midst of cutting a portly gentleman's purse when he saw Purcee. "Purcee!" he shouted, waving at the orc. The portly man turned and glared at Barry. "Purcee!" squeaked Barry, running from the man and over to his friend.

Instantly, Clarisse's hand went to the hilt of her sword, drawing it an inch to show gleaming steel. Purcee threw his arms out, almost knocking over Ted. "Barry!" he bellowed.

"I was worried about you!" said Barry, surprising himself. "I got down the stairs, and there was no sign of you. Only blood. I didn't know what to think. And here you are, alive and well!"

Purcee placed a gentle, but massive hand on Barry's head, patting him. "Barry safe. Purcee happy."

The portly man caught up to Barry, but faltered as he took in the sight of the enormous orc paladin. "You there, guard!" he said to Clarisse. "That... that man, or whatever he is... he was trying to steal from me!"

Ted sauntered over with all the grace and swagger that could be afforded to a man who had just moments prior almost had his head knocked off by a jubilant orc. "Purcee, is this your friend? Berry, or something like that? It seems as though he's nothing but a petty thief."

"Barry not petty thief."

"Yeah I'm not petty."

"There be misun, misund, misunnder…"

"You mean misunderstanding?" Barry helped.

"Yes, there misunderstanding."

Ted shook his head. "Purcee, this upstanding gentleman caught your 'friend' red-handed. I'm afraid you've been taken in by a common rogue."

"No…"

"Clarisse, arrest the halfling." Clarisse sighed and grabbed Barry by the scruff.

"I know this must be hard for you, Purcee, but justice must be served, don't you think? We'll make sure he gets a… fair trial." Ted gestured for Clarisse to move.

# PART NINE, A 'FAIR' TRIAL

Before they entered the council chambers, Ted grabbed Barry from Clarisse. He pushed open the doors and threw Barry to the ground. "This halfling was accosting the upper class in the market. He attempted to rob one of our most esteemed citizens. I thought it my civil duty, as the new captain of the guard, to bring him before you, so you might pursue justice."

"You brought us a pickpocket, to deliberate?"

"Yes. Believe me, councilors, this is important," said Ted, a glint in his eye.

"Very well then... Were there any witnesses to this crime?"

"Yes, your honours!" The portly gentleman stepped forward, puffing out his chest. "I saw everything. I was the victim of this depraved individual."

"Well then, do tell us what happened. Spare no detail, citizen."

"Well, it all started when I awoke this morning. The sun was pouring through my balcony window, casting a lovely orange light over my satin bed sheets. My maid brought me my usual breakfast, bacon and peacock eggs, with a pitcher of chilled Crystopian apple juice. None of that Brundan bilgewater for me, no sir. A chiffchaff sung outside my window as I ate..."

"Could you perhaps skip ahead, to when the crime actually took place?"

"Oh, yes, of course. Well, I had decided to go for a walk through the market, as I often do on mornings when I have no business to attend to. I did have a dilemma trying to decide between my emerald robe, and my more subdued burgundy robe. My manservant had recommended the burgundy, but I rather think my maid has better taste in fashion, and she assured me that I looked quite dashing in the emerald. There was also the question of shoes. No gentleman worth his weight in gold, as I am many times over, would be so remiss as to wear satin loafers with an emerald robe..."

"Sir, please, are the details of how you dressed yourself this morning really relevant?"

"Ah, perhaps not. My apologies, councilmen. So, as I was walking through the market, I came across a stall I had not frequented before, one which was selling highly detailed brass figurines, of which I took a fancy to. I was reminded of my maid, who just the previous week had been telling me of her suitor, who was something of an artist himself. I had dismissed it at the time, thinking little of such practice. I assured her that she would be better to court a man with a more productive role in society, but I need not tell you of the follies of young love..."

"Thank the gods," murmured one of the councillors, burying his head in his arms.

"...A young man myself, and quite dashing too, if you would still believe it. I was, at that time, courting the affections of a young lady from a lesser house than mine, but whose beauty was unparalleled. She had, against her family's wishes, taken a position of acolyte at the temple of Tyr, tending to the beautiful topiaries that once grew there. However, pious as she was, she was still a woman, and I, a man. We kissed for the first time under a shrub in the shape of a noble eagle..."

"Tell us again, why this important?"

"...A hundred years before, our families had been one, but a schism had occurred, driving brother against brother, parent against child. My grandfather had been the eldest, and most noble son, and her grandmother had been the only daughter, who had rebelled against the family's wishes and eloped with an adventuring swordsman. Pah! A mere mercenary, if you ask me. Two of her brothers, led astray by their love for her, had rallied behind her cause. And so, a civil war began, one that would tear one great house into two..."

"For the love of Bhaal and all that's unholy. It's like history class again." One of councillors had fallen asleep. The others seemed on the verge of joining him.

"...A legendary sword, given to him by a spirit of the sea, who was said to take the form of a seal in water, but that of a beautiful woman on land. This seal-maiden had been taken captive by a local fisherman, who longed to make her his wife. He kept her on land, preventing her from returning to her seal form. After the adventurer freed her from the the spell that kept her landbound, she plunged herself into the sea, returning only to bring the sword of legend, and a prophecy from the goddess Sælsïr..."

"I really don't think this is pertinent information! All we need to know is how..."

"...By a renowned blacksmith, the best on the island! It was said that this sword could slay even a god. But that, of course, might simply be legend. What we do know is that this sword was made of such fine metal, and with such expertise, that whoever wielded it was granted an enormous boon simply on the merits of the sword alone. Its edge was as sharp as moonlight, and its point was..."

"What about your point?! What is the point of all of this?!" The councillor was now red in the face, his hands gripping the edge of the podium, his knuckles white.

"...And it was just as I was leaning in to admire the statuette of this druid, that I noticed a faint tugging at my belt. I turned around, and caught the thief with his knife at my purse!"

"Wait, what? We actually... that actually went somewhere? Well, erm, can you point to the man who you caught thieving?" The man pointed a chubby finger at Barry.

"You, halfling, what was your name again?"

"His name is Berry." Ted spoke.

"Jerry, we find you guilty as charged. The punishment for theft... is death."

"That's a serious sentence, Purcee. But, I suppose, justice must be served..." Ted whispered. "I might be able to help him, get his punishment lessened. If you were willing to be more... cooperative..."

"No," said Purcee.

"No?" said Ted.

"No?" squeaked Barry.

"No. Justice must be served."

"If you think I'm bluffing…"

"You are a thief." Purcee turned to the councilors. "You are all thieves."

The councillors turned to Purcee. "What did you say?"

"Tyr knows your crimes."

"We are the law here."

"You are not justice."

"Captain, dispose of this paladin!"

Ted drew his sword, the other guards followed his lead. "Well, Purcee, I had high hopes for you. But I suppose this just isn't going to work out. Crystopian apple trees grow strong, because the ones that don't fall in line, are-" Before Ted could finish his sentence, Clarisse thrust her dagger through the back of his head. "I hate it when he talks about apples."

Clarisse cut Barry's bindings and returned his knives. "I'm a paladin of Tyr, just like you, Purcee." Purcee lifted up his axe. The guards closed in from each side. Barry, Purcee, and Clarisse went back to back, fending off their attackers.

"Guards!" screamed a councillor. "Kill them! Kill them all!" The councillors retreated into their meeting room.

"No need to kill." Purcee addressed the guards. "Your council corrupt."

"Yeah, what he said." Barry chipped in.

"Tyr only wants to root out the injustice and corruption," Clarisse added. "Tyr will spare you, just drop your weapons."

"Or we have need to kill." Purcee concluded. The guards looked at eachother and dropped their weapons. "Now leave," Purcee ordered.

Barry looked up at Purcee. "So, uh, that thing about punishing theft with death..."

"Did you steal?"

"Well, uh… I might have tried to..."

"Never again, Barry."

"Yes, okay. Sure. Definitely. Never again."

They moved up to the councillors' meeting room. When they opened the door, they could see the councillors in a circle chanting to Bhaal, attempting to summon something to protect them. From the middle of the circle a wraith appeared, it wore a red cloak and had no face to be seen underneath it.

"You have failed Bhaal." The words echoed around the room. The wraith lifted its hand and the councillors rose into the air. They screamed and begged, but the Wraith would not listen. It dropped its hand and they fell to the floor, now empty shells. "Paladins of Tyr," the wraith called out to Purcee and Clarisse. "We shall be coming for you soon, after your god is nothing but dust." The wraith disappeared, back to where it had come from.

"Well, that was anticlimactic," Barry concluded.

# PART TEN, CLARISSE'S PLAN

"So, what's another paladin of Tyr doing so far from the Citadel of Justice?" Clarisse asked Purcee.

"Purcee follow path of justice."

"So Tyr told you to come out here?"

"Yes."

"And you didn't ask why?"

"No."

"Well, if what that wraith was saying is true, we need to get back to the Citadel before this turns into an all out war."

"Will we be safe there?" Barry asked.

"Citadel could be attacked., Purcee responded.

"Well then, instead of going into one of the largest mountains in the realm to get to this Citadel of yours, I suggest we go to the inn." Purcee and Clarisse stared at Barry. "It was just an idea... just a good idea."

"I suggest we go down to the mountain from the east, and move around it to enter the Citadel via the northern tunnels," said Clarisse.

"Purcee agree."

"Whilst we are discussing what to do, does anyone have a bandage?" Barry asked.

"Why, Barry?" Purcee seemed confused.

"Because you have a gash in your back, Purcee, that you're bleeding out of."

"Where?"

"There." Barry pointed to the wound.

"Purcee bleeding." Purcee jabbed at the wound with his hand, and grunted.

"Jabbing it isn't going to help."

"Here, I can fix this." Clarisse took out her second sword.

"What are you going to do with that, make the cut worse?" Barry stared at the sword, on the hilt, two jewels moved, opening up to reveal eyes.

"What you trying to say there?" The sword spoke.

"What?" Barry responded.

"You think just because I'm a sword that I'm only good for cutting, or slicing, or dicing, or worse, stabbing?"

"Well, I mean, you're a sword."

"I'm a healer, and I'll have you know I have a name too."

Clarisse groaned. "Carlos, could you not pick a fight please, I need you to heal my colleague."

"Me fight, you know how much I hate fighting. I don't do any of that anymore, I'm a new sword, reformed so to say, refined. I decided that killing just isn't for me. I'm a conscientious objector, alright?"

"That's great, Carlos, but can you please do your healing thing?"

"As long as it isn't short man over here."

"No, it's the orc."

"What orc?"

"That orc." Clarisse turned the sword in her hand so Carlos could see Purcee.

"Oh the orc, yes." Carlos went bright white and Clarisse pressed him against Purcee's wound. Within seconds the wound was gone, as if it had never been there. "See? Isn't that much nicer than all that killing stuff you normally get up to?"

"You know what... I'm not even surprised anymore. A magic healing sword really isn't that outlandish compared to all the other weird things we've seen now," said Barry.

"Thank you Carlos." Clarisse put Carlos away.

"So, anyone for the inn?" Barry asked.

"No!" Said Purcee and Clarisse in unison.

"It was worth another try. To the Citadel of Justice then."

"I'd like to see the inn," spoke Carlos from his sheathe.

"See, it's two against two."

"Carlos doesn't get a vote."

"That's racist!" Carlos declared.

"You're a talking sword, you aren't part of any race."

"You don't know that, there could be more sentient swords out there. I mean have you talked to every sword in the world?"

"No, you would be the first."

"So do I get a vote then?"

"I'll do you one better." Clarisse unsheathed Carlos and placed him on the ground. "You can go to the inn, go on, it's just out that door and three streets over."

"That's very funny, cause I'm a sword and haven't

got legs. I see what you've done here and I must say I am against it on every front."

"Hey, buddy, you don't have to put up with her," said Barry, carefully picking up Carlos. "We can go to the inn together! Say, do you know how valuable you are?"

# PART ELEVEN, THE DEMON DRAGON

Suddenly, a demon dragon appeared in the sky above Crystopia, breathing plumes of deadly demon fire, igniting the rooftops and spires of the great city. I'm not exaggerating when I say that it was big. It was like two giants had a baby, and that baby ate some of the leaves of the Kindred Forest, and if that doesn't give you a sense of the scale of this beast, I don't know what will. Well actually, one of its claws was about as big as Purcee so that probably gives you an idea.

"Oh, no!" said Barry. "It's a demon dragon!"

"Before you ask, no I will not stab the demon dragon," declared Carlos.

"But-" started Barry.

"Nope."

"You-"

"Not happening."

"Are-"

"A conscientious objector."

"A sword."

"And you were made to fit in small hard to get places."

"Low blow."

"You want to make me an accessory to murder."

"You literally are the accessory to murder."

"Not today I'm not!"

"It's a demon dragon!"

"It could have a family."

"Of equally terrifying dragon demons."

"That deserve a chance to live with the peace of mind that they shan't be stabbed, not today."

"But it's burning down the city!"

"I don't care, I ain't stabbing it. Use another, dumber, non sentient sword, that hasn't taken an oath to do no harm."

Suddenly, Purcee grabbed Carlos, brandishing him over his head and running towards the demon dragon, bellowing his battle cry!

"Juuuuuuuustice-" screamed Purcee

"Ahhhhhhhhh-" cried Carlos.

Purcee and Carlos were swept into the air and sucked down the dragon's gullet.

"Purcee! No!" screamed Barry. "And also Carlos!"

"It's too late for them," said Clarisse. "We need to get out of here or we're next!"

The demon dragon clawed the floor and lava shot up, out of the flames came dragon demons - man-sized draconic monsters of stone.

"Oh no, dragon demons!" said Barry.

"I thought the big one was a dragon demon?" said Clarisse.

"No, that's a demon dragon. Dragon demons are the minions of the demon dragon."

"How do you know so much about this?"

"I took a class."

"A class?"

"Well a few classes actually, they don't just start you off on demon dragons, you know. First you've got your regular dragons, then your arch dragons, then your true dragons, then demi-dragons… don't get me started on all the subspecies. Wyverns, drakes, wyrms…"

"So you took a dragon class?"

"No, it was a cooking course actually, the lecturer just really liked dragons. She would love this if she was here, if she hadn't of had the accident."

"Did she get eaten by a dragon?"

"No, she tried to cook fugu, but messed it up."

"Look, this doesn't matter, we have to fight these demon dragon things now!"

"Dragon demons! Pay attention!"

The dragon demons encircled Barry and Clarisse. For a few seconds everything stopped. Then, the first dragon demon lunged. The others all followed. Clarisse cut through the first like paper: leathery, flame spewing, death loving, extremely coarse paper. The second dragon demon bit into her arm, she punched it and stabbed it in the gut, it started bleeding lava.

Barry was dodging the bites, he got underneath one and managed to jab his knife into its belly, but when he tried to pull it out it was stuck, and lava was leaking out of the wound. Barry rolled out leaving the knife. Clarisse and Barry re-joined, but they were being backed into a wall. There were too many dragon demons. Suddenly in the sky above a great white light shot out of the demon dragon's mouth. It swooped down and crashed onto the floor of the city square. The demon dragon lifted its head up and light shot into the air, dancing over the mountains and beyond.

"It has to be Purcee! He has his smite back! This demon dragon doesn't know who it's dealing with."

"That's no smite," said Clarisse.

Suddenly the light ceased. The demon dragon grumbled and regurgitated Purcee and Carlos.

"Oh yeah, healers one, killers none." Carlos declared.

"You healed the murder dragon?!" Clarisse exclaimed.

The demon dragon made a sound, almost like a purr, and then proceeded to lick Purcee and Carlos affectionately.

"Dragon had bad stomach." Purcee explained.

"You're saying it had indigestion?" Barry asked.

"Ohh… we murdered so many dragon demons there…" Clarisse stuttered.

"That's okay, it just forms them out of stone."

The demon dragon purred once again. It turned and took flight.

"Well, the demon dragon is defeated, and Crystopia is now safe from corrupt governments and the oblivion of death. I say we've earnt a trip to the inn." Barry concluded.

"I'm all up for that idea." Carlos agreed.

"The inn got burnt down." Clarisse pointed to the rubble.

"Damn you, demon dragon!" cursed Barry.

"If we leave now we should arrive at the citadel in less than a month." Clarisse started moving, Purcee followed.

"I hope the citadel has an inn." Barry whined.

# PART TWELVE, THE CITADEL OF JUSTICE

The citadel was one of those places that Barry wasn't too keen on. There were too many stairs for one; and the nearest tavern was all the way back down the mountain.

"I wish you'd told me there wasn't a tavern up here before we, you know, climbed up here." Barry complained.

"Why would we need a tavern?" Clarisse asked.

"You know, for fun, and to be social, and to drink."

"Why don't we go find the Grandmaster?" Clarisse suggested, "It's just up those stairs."

"Why is it that all your temples and citadels and Grandmasters are all up so many stairs?"

"It good for legs." Purcee spoke.

"Hey, not all of us have legs." Carlos interjected.

"Well, we aren't all as lucky as you Carlos. I wish my paladin had carried me up the stairs."

When they entered the offices for the Masters of Justice they saw a massive rock on a pedestal to the centre, as they moved around it they saw the reception area and some waiting chairs. Clarisse and Purcee walked up to the reception.

"Appointment?!" barked the receptionist.

"Well, erm, no, we don't, we were hoping the Grand-master was..." Barry stammered.

"No one sees the Grandmaster without an appointment!"

"What is she, her bouncer?" Barry whispered.

"You think justice is deaf, halfing?"

"No, maam."

"I am the holy receptionist of mighty justice, and none shall pass... without an appointment."

"Uh-huh..."

"I want to see your paladin identifications, all of you."

Clarisse was first to have her papers out. The receptionist looked them over and did a short nod. "And you, halfing?"

"Oh, I'm not a paladin, I'm just with them."

"Hmm, and you, orc?"

"My name Purcee."

"Purcee?"

"Purcee."

"The Purcee?"

"Purcee."

"As in the highest scoring graduate in the arena of justice since the creation of the order? That Purcee?"

"Purcee." Purcee nodded.

"I knew you looked familiar. My, oh my, you've gotten so big since the last time I saw you. You was only double my height then."

"So, seeing as how my friend Purcee is such a big deal around here... do you think you could let us in without an appointment?"

"Um… no."

"Could we make an appointment?"

"…Yes."

"Great! Okay! When for? When's the soonest appointment?"

"In about… three months."

"Three months?! But we need to see the Grandmaster today!"

"I mean, that's the civilian appointments, there is a different diary for paladin appointments."

"That's good. Can you look in that one?"

"…No."

"Why not?"

"Because you're not a paladin."

"Well, I don't need to be in the meeting. Just them."

"I would have to book it with them, then."

"Fine."

"I'm afraid no civilian can be present to know anything in the paladin diary."

"Really?"

"Yes."

"I guess I'll go sit over there."

"This not take long, Barry." Purcee reassured.

"This is so unfair," Barry mumbled walking away, "Carlos isn't a paladin and he's allowed to hear what's in the paladin diary."

"Who's Carlos?" The receptionist asked.

"Oh, that's just my sentient sword." Clarisse answered.

The receptionist raised an eyebrow.

"Barry, come back here and take Carlos with you."

Barry grabbed Carlos and headed over to the seats.

"Hey, man, where's the nearest inn?"

"Down about ten miles of stairs."

"Ah man, who makes a citadel and doesn't put a tavern in it anywhere."

"That's what I said!"

"Paladins, am I right?"

"Wait a second, what is it about inns that you like so much? I mean it can't be the drinking."

"Hey, swords like to socialise too, and where better to socialise than an inn?"

"I don't know. Maybe where swords usually socialise."

"And where's that then?"

"Armory for the introverts, battlefield for the extroverts?"

"Why don't you just find a blacksmith's shop and leave me there for a few hours then!"

"You could use a polish."

"How dare you."

"Appointment booked." Purcee sat down next to Barry.

"When for?"

"Ten minutes."

"Wait, so it's three months for civilians, but ten minutes for paladins? That doesn't seem very just. I mean, how many civilians want to climb up a mountain?"

"Ten thousand, six hundred and four."

"What?"

Clarisse sat down, "ten thousand six hundred and

four, there's been a surge in appointments since the cult of Bhaal started their crusade."

"Oh, okay then." They all sat quietly waiting to be called for their appointment. Barry was getting uncomfortable. He hated silence, why wasn't anyone talking, not even Carlos? What was going on. The silence had been going on for far too long now but due to that Barry felt that anything that he would say to break the silence would have to be of great importance. An idea suddenly blossomed in his mind. He had it, a perfect sliver of small talk that would allow escape from this purgatory, this liminality between conversations. "So, erm. That's a big rock."

"That's just the boulder of desire." Clarisse sighed.

"The what what of what?"

"Boulder of desire." Purcee said.

"And what does it do?"

"When you touch it the boulder will tell you what you truly desire." Clarisse explained. Purcee stood up and walked over to the boulder, he laid his hand on it and the boulder echoed one word. "Justice." Purcee smiled and returned to his seat. "Purcee true."

Clarisse went next. "Peace," echoed the boulder.

"Wow, that's so cool! I want a go, someone let me have a go!" Carlos begged. Clarisse grabbed Carlos and touched him to the stone. "SLAUGHTER! MURDER! DEATH AND DESTRUCTION! SUBJUGATION OF THE MORTAL RACES!"

"Nope, no, no. I don't want that. Obviously this stupid rock doesn't work on sentient swords. I have made a lifestyle choice not to do that, no matter how much I want to, cause murder is wrong, it's just, it's wrong."

"Barry, you go." Said Purcee.

"Um… that's okay. I know it will just say 'justice', or 'peace', or something like that… Something nice and not at all illegal."

"The Grandmaster of the guild will now see Paladins Clarisse and Purcee," the receptionist called. Purcee and Clarisse headed in for the meeting, leaving Barry and Carlos in the reception.

"I wonder what the Grandmaster looks like." Barry wondered.

"Eh, she ain't that impressive."

"Wait, you've seen her?"

"Yeah."

"And what was she like?"

"Well, she wasn't a sword."

"I'd guessed that."

"Oh, so just because she's the Grandmaster she can't be a sword?"

"Carlos, you are the only sentient sword I have ever met. You could be the only one in existence for all I know."

"Nah, man, there's my cousin Fred. He was the runt of the litter though."

"The litter? You mean you were… born? I don't even want to think about that."

"We were forged by a powerful Enchanter, imbued with world altering powers. But with great power comes great sentience apparently."

"How many of you are there?"

"Well, there's me, and Fred… and, yeah that's all I've

got."

"So… did you just get the average power, then?"

"I am a healer like no other, created to keep armies from falling to the undead. When I was at full strength I could obliterate an undead army at a hundred thousand strong."

"Wait, so you killed them?"

"Well, they were already dead. Healing the undead has the opposite effect to healing the living."

"I still think that counts as killing them."

"Hey, I'm a changed sword now though, I only heal these days."

"So wait, if you were made to destroy the undead, what was Fred made for?"

"Cutting onions without inflicting tears."

"Are you serious?"

"No, of course not, I only ever saw Fred once. I don't know what he does"

"What did he look like?"

"Well, he was a bit small for a sword."

"So a dagger?"

"A dagger, yes, but like a kitchen dagger."

"A cutting knife?"

"Yes, but for opening mail."

"So… a letter opener."

"Yeah, but in the kitchen."

"Did the Enchanter always open his mail in the kitchen?"

"Yeah, with Fred. He was always good for cutting them letters open."

"Surely all knives would be good for that?"

"All but me."

"Because you made a lifestyle…"

"A lifestyle choice!"

"Yeah, I get it." Barry looked over at the rock. "Carlos?"

"Yeah?"

"If I were to… touch that rock… you wouldn't tell the others what it said, would you?"

"Why, is it going to say something bad?"

"No worse than 'death, destruction, and subjugation of the mortal races!'"

"Hey, hey, it clearly doesn't work on swords!"

"Right. Well, I'm going to go touch that stone." Barry walked over to the stone and extended his hand, his fingers almost brushing the surface of the rock. He hesitated.

"Are you scared of the rock?"

"No! I was just… wondering if it was valuable…" Barry mumbled.

"What did you say?"

"Nothing incriminating! I'm touching it now." Barry touched the stone.

"Wealth. Riches!" boomed the stone.

"Your greatest desire is to be rich?! Some hero you are."

"I just to be want to be rich so that I can… give to the needy! Share my wealth with the world."

"Personal wealth!" the stone boomed again, with Barry's hand still pressed against it.

"Well, this is awkward." Carlos spoke.

"As awkward as this." Barry touched Carlos to the

rock.

"TOTAL OBLITERATION, A THOUSAND YEARS OF SUFFERING AS AN APPETIZER, BLOOD, CARNAGE, DEAAAAAAAATH!"

Purcee and Clarisse walked out. "What are you two doing?"

"Nothing." Barry claimed. "Don't say anything." He whispered to Carlos.

"No time to waste, let's get going." Clarisse ordered taking Carlos back from Barry.

"Where are we going, boss?" Carlos asked.

"Down the mountain and..."

"To the tavern?" Barry interjected.

"Oh yeah, the tavern, that would be good." Carlos agreed.

"No, we are going past the tavern and to the plains of Abidurval."

"Wait, what?" shrieked Carlos.

"Abidurval." Purcee helped.

"I know what that is, but why are we going there of all places?" Carlos shrieked.

"We're taking you home, Carlos."

"What! No thank you, don't do that. The Enchanter, he is crazy, loopy, he always said if he ever saw me again he would take away my sentience."

"Why would he ever do that?" asked Barry.

"He didn't approve of me being a conscientious objector. I don't want to die Clarisse, don't do this. I beg you."

"Carlos, this isn't up for discussion."

"How about we split into two teams, a strike team

with you and Purcee…"

"Strike team." Purcee repeated.

"…and a secondary team, of me and Barry, as a reserve for you, so to say. We could stay in a headquarters and we can strategize."

"And where would these headquarters be? In the inn?" Clarisse glared unflinchingly.

"Erm… no."

Clarisse's glare intensified.

"Okay, yes, yes it would have been."

"We are going to the Enchanter, we will get what we need and don't worry, we won't let him lay a finger on you."

# PART THIRTEEN, THE PATH TO THE ENCHANTER

Barry swung Carlos around in a circle. "So, which way Carlos?" Barry asked.

"I'm not telling."

"That way?" Barry turned Carlos to point north.

"Not even close."

"How about that way." Barry pointed east towards the mountains.

"Yeah, the plains of Abidurval are atop some mountains."

"It could be a plateau."

"Well it's the opposite of that."

"A hole?"

"No, flat! It is flat. That's why it's called the plains of Abidurval, not the mountain of Abidurval or the ocean of Abidurval or the slightly hilly front of Abidurval."

"What about..." Barry spun the sword around again stopping it pointing southwards. "That way?"

"That's the Citadel of Justice. We just came from there."

"So that's a no, then?"

"Yes."

"What does that leave us with?"

"West." Purcee chimed in.

"Yes, west, thank you. That's what I've been saying all along. It is west, right buddy?"

"Yes. it's west."

"Then we go west!" Barry said, marching east.

Purcee gently grabbed Barry by the collar, turning him to face westwards. Barry continued walking as though nothing had happened, and Purcee and Clarisse followed after him.

"So how far are these plains?" asked Barry.

"About five hundred miles."

"Five hundred miles?!"

"Yeah, so it's not far." Carlos said.

"Maybe not to you! You're not the one who has to walk it all! How long will it take?"

Clarisse looked down at Barry. "For me and Purcee... just over two weeks, if we make good time. But for you..."

"What do you mean, 'for me'?"

"Well, your legs..."

"What? They're short? Is that what you're going to say? That I have short legs?"

"Yes."

"Well... well, uh... You have long legs!"

"Thank you." Clarisse walked past Barry, signalling the end of the discussion.

"Hey, Purcee?" said Barry.

"Yes, Barry?"

"...Carry me?"

"No, Barry," said Purcee, as he carried on after Clarisse.

"What? Why not?"

"Exercise."

"Exercise?"

"You need exercise. To grow legs."

Barry spluttered. "You… you think if I exercise, my legs will grow?"

"Worked for Purcee."

"Unbelievable…" said Barry, still clutching Carlos.

"You better hurry, or they'll leave you behind," said the sword. "But don't go too fast! You wouldn't want to get… short of breath…"

"I don't know what you're laughing about. At least I have legs!"

Barry hurried after the two paladins, swinging Carlos around over his head.

"Stop it! You're making me nauseous…"

"We've got a long road ahead of us, my metal friend. You're just going to have to get used to it."

"I think I'm going to be sick…"

"I don't think that's possible."

\*\*\*

The next three weeks were long and arduous, but otherwise uneventful, unless you count the rogue griffon attack, the water nymph run-in, or the pygmy bandit showdown. The pygmy bandits were bandits who stole pygmies, rather than bandits who were pygmies. They'd mistook Barry for a pygmy and tried to steal him, but their efforts were thwarted by a rival group of bandit pygmies. Other than those incidents, the most notable moment of the journey was when Purcee stubbed his toe and caused a rockslide. But, at long last, the party found themselves at their destination: the Plains of Abidurval.

"…I don't see any plains," said Barry.

# PART FOURTEEN, THE VERY FLAT PLAINS OF ABIDURVAL

As Carlos looked at his home a feeling of dread rubbed against him like a polishing cloth. "That was definitely not like that before."

The Plains of Abidurval looked exactly the way you'd expect plains to look. Grassy fields, pleasant hills, grazing sheep. The only thing that was a little unusual was the fact that they were entirely vertical. It was like someone had plucked the land from the ground and left it to hang from some invisible, celestial hook. The sheep didn't seem to notice their geometrical predicament, carrying on as though everything were normal and all was right with the world, when in fact all was right-angled with the world. In summation, it was a whole load of messed up.

"So, that's a whole load of messed up." concluded Barry. "I thought you said they were flat."

"Well, they are flat, just in a vertical fashion." Carlos argued.

"When people say flat, they kind of think horizontal."

"They do?"

"Yes."

"Well, it wasn't like this last time."

"How do we get over there?"

"Ladder," said Purcee.

From the tip of the Enchanter's tower was a ladder, imbedded into the cliff about ten feet down. That would be ten Barry feet though, not ten Purcee feet, it'd be below the clouds in that case.

"Ah, so there is. We could walk along it and reach the roof of the tower."

"Good plan," Clarisse agreed. "You should go first, Barry, and Purcee last."

"What, why?"

"Because you're the lightest and Purcee's the heaviest."

"I'm not going first! Are you crazy?"

"It makes sense, Barry. If you didn't want to go into the tower why did you come with us?"

"No one told me the tower would be, would be…"

"Floating?" Clarisse finished.

"Yes!"

"Enough talk." Purcee declared, leaping off the cliff. As he fell onto the ladder the gravity shifted. His foot caught the ladder and he grabbed on tight.

"Gravity odd." Purcee shouted, staring up at the rest, who were looking straight at him.

"Just stand up on the ladder and walk there." Clarisse ordered.

"Purcee can not stand."

"Why?"

"Purcee is stood on ladder."

"What?"

"Erm, guys," Carlos spoke. "I think what Purcee is trying to say is that gravity doesn't work over there like it works over here."

"Doesn't work?"

"Well not like doesn't work, but works in a kind of freaky way."

"So, down is down here, but once we leave this cliff, down matches the plains?" Barry asked.

"Yeah."

"Well then, I have a way to test this." Clarisse grabbed some rope out of her bag and tied it around a tree. She fastened the other end around herself.

"What are you doing with that?" Barry asked.

"You'll see." Clarisse ran and jumped forwards off the cliff. She started to fall towards the ladder but then gravity swapped for her and she hung above the tower waiting to be lowered. From Barry's perspective she was floating a few meters off the cliff, but from her perspective it was the cliff now that was on its side.

"I'm going to climb down."

"How? You're flying!"

"From your point of view I may be." Clarisse steadily lowered herself onto the balcony of the tower. Purcee clambered down the ladder and joined her.

"Come Barry, it okay." Purcee said looking up at Barry.

"Erm, no. I'm good here where down is down and not across."

"Barry, get down here. We need Carlos!"

"Oh, I see how it is." Barry reluctantly climbed down the rope.

# PART FIFTEEN, THE MAD ENCHANTER

They entered the tower and found themselves in an elegant room with carpeted floors, intricately-engraved wooden furniture, and a stunning four-pronged crystal chandelier that hung from the ceiling. It was a very sharp chandelier that was casting a shadow on the ground, four shadows to be precise. In front of them was a glowing sword held in place by metallic arms pointed to the right. Barry went over to look at it.

"This looks valuable." He reached out to touch it.

"Don't touch that, halfing."

"Huh," spoke Barry. "Who said that? Clarisse, was that you?"

"I didn't hear anything." Clarisse replied.

A faint chanting started. It emanated from the next room over. Clarisse snuck over to the door. She looked at Barry and put a finger over her mouth. She opened the door to see a monk sat on the floor, cross-legged and chanting.

"Are you the Enchanter?" Clarisse asked but received no response.

"Nah," Carlos answered, "that's just the chanter. How's things, Steve?" The man nodded. "Could you go find the big guy for us, Steve?" The man stood up, bowed his head and left. "Okay, Steve is going to go grab the Enchanter. If the Enchanter tries to take me, I want you to thrown me out of the window, Clarisse."

"What, why would we do that?"

"Because I would fall into the fires beneath the plains, and surely be destroyed. Death is a better alternative than non sentience."

"Wouldn't both of those alternatives mean your death?" Barry interrupted.

"Well, let's hope it doesn't come to that."

"Hello again, Carlos." Spoke a giant hooded figure. "You returned home."

"You must be the Enchanter." Clarisse spoke. "We need something from you."

"And why would I be likely to assist you?"

"To save the world."

"I've saved the world. I gave that bow on the wall to the king of Admenia to allow him to teleport into the plain of his enemy. I gave Carlos to the Citadel of Justice to defeat the hordes of the non-living. I made Steve to chant so we might calm the fires below the Plains of Abidurval. What next, why must the world be saved again?"

"From Bhaal." Purcee declared.

"Bhaal just wants the death of all sentience, the world will be fine."

"We were told you had a weapon, a sword that can kill a god."

"That weapon is here."

"In this room?" Clarisse looked around.

"Yes."

Clarisse picked up a sword with a red tempered blade. "This looks like a god killer. Is this the weapon we seek?"

"You posses the weapon you seek."

"Ah, that was easier than I thought." Clarisse sheathed the sword on her back. "You're okay with us just taking this sword, right?"

"On one condition. You give Carlos back to me."

"No, Clarisse, you can't."

"Not going to happen."

"I wasn't requesting." The Enchanter turned to the pedestal and touched the glowing sword and turned it downwards. Everyone started to float and the plains began to shift. From above the fires beneath the plains became visible. The sword locked into place and the plains stopped moving. Everyone returned to the ground. "I shall throw Carlos back to the fires from whence he came."

"Over my dead body." Clarisse declared.

"That was the plan." The Enchanter took a coin from his pocket and whispered to it. He then threw it at Clarisse. Her reflexes caught it before she could think. As it touched her skin the artificial gravity lost its effect on her. She fell up the room and hit into the wall, she clawed the bow from the wall before smashing through the glass ceiling. Clarisse notched an arrow as she fell into the fires of Abidurval. She thought if she were to die, she would take the Enchanter with her. She shot the arrow, it rose up from the flames, down into the tower and narrowly missed the Enchanter before it imbedded in the floor beneath him.

"Oh no." The Enchanter spoke as the bow recalled. Clarisse teleported back into the room and the bow notched against its arrow. As she fell again she touched the coin to the Enchanter's skin and pulled him off the ground. Purcee grabbed Clarisse's arm, and the Enchanter tried to grab her leg to save himself. Clarisse kicked him, but he clutched tighter, digging his perfectly-manicured nails into her flesh. She shook and kicked him again. His grip lessened and he fell impaling himself on the chandelier at the top of the room.

"We did it." Carlos celebrated. "He's dead, and I'm still alive, and sentient."

"We're going to die." Steve screamed, he pointed at the glowing sword, its light was fading.

"Set it straight." Carlos shouted to Barry. Barry turned the sword upwards and the plains began to shift. The sword's glow was fading more and more, and the artificial gravity was fading with it. They started to fall towards the fires. Purcee managed to grab the ladder and threw Clarisse against it. Purcee then grabbed Barry but Steve fell, screaming into oblivion.

"Steve! No!" yelled Carlos. The flames grew harsher now the chanter was silent.

The ladder scraped against the cliff as the plains returned to its original ninety degree offset. The group began running across the ladder attempting to reach the cliff edge. The plains didn't stop at the ninety degree offset, determined to realign with the rest of the world. Running became climbing as they got higher and higher. They were almost at the cliff when the ladder made a sound, and then another one closer to a shriek.

"The ladder is going to break." Clarisse screamed just before it snapped. They fell downwards and through the gap between the plains and the cliff. The gap closed behind them as the plains fully realigned. Above them was naught but darkness and below was the light of the flames. The fires were roaring, waiting to be fed. Over the crackle came a screech. It became louder and louder. The ground above them shattered and the demon dragon flew down, it grabbed them in its claws and carried them out. It raced through the sky and past the tower. Below they could see the sword's glow extinguish and as it did the plains dropped into the fires of Abidurval. The sheep spread wings and took to the skies, as the tower sunk slowly into the depths.

The demon dragon dropped them on the cliffside. Purcee hugged it and patted it's snout.

"Good evil dragon. You good evil dragon."

"How'd it know to come for us?" Clarisse asked.

"She good evil dragon."

"Dragons don't like being indebted to people." Barry explained. "Purcee and Carlos saved her life, she wouldn't have been truly free until she'd done the same. She's probably been following us since Crystopia."

"She good evil dragon." Purcee nodded.

"Or what he said I guess."

# PART SIXTEEN, NOT EVERY GOD IS BOTHERED WITH SIMPLE MORALITY

"At least we have a ride back to The Citadel of Justice." Carlos said. The Demon Dragon licked Purcee and flew away.

"Why dragon go?" Purcee asked.

"She paid back her debt," said Barry.

"Guess we're walking then," Carlos informed.

"Easy for you to say, you get carried."

"Actually, myself and Carlos will be taking a quicker route. We were ordered to return with the sword as promptly as possible, remember?" Clarisse notched her bow and fired. The arrow flew five hundred meters before embedding into the ground. Clarisse and Carlos disappeared, reappearing at her arrow. She waved from the distance before doing the same again.

"Guess it's just us again, buddy." Barry said.

"Friends." Purcee replied.

"...Carry me?"

Purcee picked Barry up and placed him on his shoulder. "No telling Clarisse."

"I don't suppose you have any more dragon friends, do you?"

"No, Barry."

"Well, I guess we're walking then..." They began to move, it took them a lot longer to go five hundred meters than Clarisse with her stupid, really convenient, take-you-where-you-wanna-go-bow. "So, Purcee, how long have you been a paladin?"

"Two hundred and twenty winters next snow."

"Two hundred and twenty? How old are you?"

"Two hundred and forty nine snows."

"Wait, you do know that it can snow multiple times in a year, right?"

"Snow many time in year?"

"Yeah, like it snowed four times so far this year."

"It did?"

"Yeah, and in different places it can snow more or less in a year."

"But when get cold, when come snow, that is winter."

"Purcee, I'm not sure you quite understand the passage of time; you can't be two hundred and twenty, orcs don't live that long. Wait, what is the lifespan of an orc?"

"Purcee young orc."

"Are most orcs you've seen younger or older than you."

"Younger."

"So that would make you an old orc."

"They my age."

"Then how would they be younger?"

"Died in battle."

"What battle?"

"Big battle."

"Against?"

"Evil."

Suddenly a tear appeared in front of them. From it walked a man with incredibly normal features. You wouldn't be able to pick him out of a line up if last year's harvest depended on it.

"You are Purcee and Barry, adventurers, fighters of evil, and friends?" The man spoke, his voice was as monotonous as his appearance. "Fear not my appearance, nor my voice."

Barry looked around in confusion. "Erm… were you talking to us?"

"Yes. Who else is here?" Some sheep flew overhead.

"What did you say? I don't think I caught it."

"I said not to fear my appearance, nor my voice." Barry looked at the man, blankly. "I am not like your god, Tyr. Nor am I like Bhaal. I'm the one in between, the Godellfriar of Order. I am… Geoff."

"Sorry, what? There's just something about your voice that makes me… not want to pay attention. Start from the beginning, and I promise I'll listen. You have my full and undivided attention."

Geoff glared at Barry. "I said I am not like the gods of good or the gods of evil. I am the one in between."

"…In between what?"

"In between the other gods!" Geoff stated.

"Oh! You had a bit of emotion there."

"No, I didn't!"

"Right, okay, okay. I'm sorry. Let's start over. What was your name?"

"I am the one called Geoff, Godellfriar of Order."

"Jeff? That's a bit… That's not very godly, is it? I know lots of Jeffs."

"They were named after me."

"Wait, I've always wanted to know, which way do you spell Jeff?"

"The correct way, G-E-O-F-F."

"Oh, so what about the people who named their kids Jeff with a J? Are those kids named after you too?"

"Yes, but their parents are illiterate."

"Uh-huh. So who are you?"

"This is going nowhere! Silence!" Geoff raised his hand and Barry's mouth was sealed shut. "I will speak to the smart one," said Geoff, looking at Purcee.

"Purcee," said Purcee.

"Yes, I know."

"Geoff," said Purcee.

"Yes, that is me."

"Purcee."

"Oh dear. Purcee, it's come to my attention that you and your associates are trying to to stop the return of Bhaal. I'm afraid I cannot let you do that."

"Bhaal bad."

"Yes, but so is Tyr."

"Purcee not understand."

"Worlds need balance. Bhaal will turn this world into a realm of chaos. Tyr will turn it into a world of justice."

"Justice good."

"Some justice, but Tyr always goes too far, step on a bug and accept the same fate. Such is just to him."

"Tyr is true."

"Tyr is too true. One cannot live in a state of chaos or justice. There must be order."

"Mmf mm Mmmffmm mmf mmfmmff?" said Barry.

"What is it, halfling?" Geoff raised his hand and Barry could speak once more.

"So if Clarisse kills Bhaal, what happens?"

"Tyr breaks into this realm and kills anyone who has ever done a slight injustice."

"Well... that would suck. For those people who have been unjust..."

"You be fine Barry, you just." said Purcee.

"Thanks, Purcee. I'm just worried about all the people in the world who are a little unjust but are still good people... People who just want to get rich off of others, but still have good hearts, you know? Deep down, I think they're good. I'm worried about those sorts of people..."

"Barry, Tyr is just, it would be quick. Painless. They would become memories."

"I don't want to become a memory!"

"You fine, Barry. You just."

"Purcee, I'm sorry to tell you this, but I'm not just. I'm actually very unjust. The first time we met, I was trying to rob you! I've tried to steal from everyone we've met. Even right now I'm looking at Geoff for things to steal."

"You couldn't steal from me," said Geoff.

"That's because you have nothing worth stealing, you boring old coot! Purcee, I'm not just. I don't think

I'm a very good person at all. I only wanted to travel with you at first because I knew I could use you to make myself rich. If you knew even the half of my injustice, you'd smite me yourself. I certainly won't stand a chance if Tyr comes into our world."

"You know Barry, being dead. It not so bad. I died once."

"You did?"

"I felt cold. My body was gone, my essence floated in empty space. Purcee not feel, not think, not fear. Purcee yearned for abyss. Purcee accept, drown, and find solace. Purcee then woke. Saved by Tyr."

"I don't want to die, though."

"Death can be messy, like when your insides are outside."

"Is that what will happen to me?!"

"No Barry, your death calm, peaceful."

"Purcee... If Tyr told you to kill me, would you?"

Purcee looked at Barry. He went to speak but couldn't find the word.

"You two. Stop squabbling over death. I need you to make sure there is order in the world." Geoff stated.

"And how would we do that?"

"By not killing Bhaal."

"But if we don't, Bhaal will destroy this world."

"The world would be fine. He would kill all of you though."

"But Bhaal wants to kill Tyr. What if he succeeds?"

"Then you would need to kill Bhaal."

"Order?" Purcee asked.

"Look, there can be both of them or neither. In the

end order will prevail."

"And if it doesn't?"

"I'll be honest with you mortals, the odds for your survival don't look good. If Bhaal wins, you all die. If Tyr wins, the unjust die, which is most of you. Either way most to all of you will die."

"Cheerful. Well, can you help us?"

"Why would I do that?"

"For your precious order?"

"I won't intervene."

"Isn't this intervening?"

"I'm only intervening now to let you know that I won't intervene."

"Then why not just not intervene at all?"

"Because I wanted you to know my intent to not intervene by slightly intervening."

"Can't you just intervene slightly more, and, you know, help us out?"

"No because then I would be intervening more than I originally intended."

"So, you don't have anything useful to offer us? No advice on averting the apocalypse?"

"Say goodbye to those you love, they are either dead, or they will wish they were."

"Well then, I think I speak for both of us when I say: go away, Geoff."

"Purcee." Purcee nodded

"We will be fine, won't we Purcee?"

"Yes."

"We don't need any stupid help from any stupid gods. Let's go, Purcee."

"Purcee." Purcee nodded.

# PART SEVENTEEN, CITADEL OUT OF WHACK

Clarisse could see the citadel. It was in flames, the cult of Bhaal surrounded it. Their army was bigger than any Clarisse had seen before. They had giants and demon dragons, a few ice wyverns and a fire atronach plus an army of grunts. There was even a fearsome flock of reverse griffons - savage creatures with the legs and tail of an eagle, and the head of a lion. You'd think they'd look a bit daft, and you'd be right, but they're also the apex predators of the Agola savannah, capable of running at speeds of tens of metres an hour, and, more importantly, of breathing reverse fire. It was these reverse griffons that were currently burning the citadel with their reverse fire, which was like regular fire, except it could not be impeded by water. Which was handy as it was currently raining a storm. One of the giants held an umbrella over the fire atronach to stop it from getting doused. The reverse fire atronach was fine however, as it was made of ice. Surely there's a better name for it.

Clarisse looked out over the armies of Bhaal, and

notched an arrow on her bow.

"Ready, Carlos?"

"Do I get a choice? You could always imbed me in a big stone and wait for a king to claim me?"

Clarisse aimed her bow towards the giant. "Oh, we're ready."

"Or you could throw me in a lake, maybe there would be a nicer lady in there."

"You'd miss me." Clarisse shot the arrow, it imbedded in the giant's skull. Clarisse was teleported to the arrow, she stabbed the red tempered blade into the giant's head. It fell with a mighty thud and with it went the umbrella. The rain started to tap against the fire atronach. It screamed a hellish cry and fell against the reverse atronach melting its ice.

Wait... ice atronach, that's a much easier name.

The ice atronach shattered, spilling liquid ice which splashed over the reverse griffons, freezing them solid. As the giant tumbled forward, Clarisse let loose another arrow, carrying her to the entrance of the Citadel. A young paladin stared at her, jaw agape. Clarisse turned to look at the swath of destruction that laid in her wake.

"Ohmygosh..." whimpered Carlos.

The battle was still far from won. The horde had taken a blow, but it wouldn't be a horde if it couldn't. Two demon dragons still circled the skies around the Citadel, sending forth their dragon demons and breathing demon fire. Giants still plodded towards the walls, with cultists marching after them. Clarisse turned back to the young paladin.

"Paladin, who's in charge of the defense? General

Tony? Grandmaster Ethel?"

"No one, ma'am. They're dead."

"They're both dead? Then who's in charge?"

"That's what I'm telling you. No one's in charge. Our defenses are already breached. All the masters have been sacrificed to Bhaal."

"Then what you're saying is..."

"We've already lost. Bhaal is returning."

As he spoke those words, a tremendous crack resonated from within the mountain. Lightning struck down from above.

"What do we do?" The paladin cried. "We're dead, we're dead, we're so dead."

"Get a hold of yourself, paladin. Do you see this?" Clarisse gestured to the red tempered blade in her hand. "This is a god killer. We got it from the Enchanter. They may bring Bhaal back, and if they do I will stab this sword through him with enough force to end him and make all the other gods quiver. Now you are going to get whatever forces we have left, and together we're going to kill a god."

The young paladin ran off into the Citadel, leaving Clarisse at the gate.

"Ready, Carlos?"

# PART EIGHTEEN, GOD AT THE GATES

A rift had opened in the centre of the mountain, through it stepped Bhaal. He was a giant, his eyes were red, his armour stained black from the ashes of his plain.

"I bring chaos to this land. I will free you from the melancholy of life."

Glenn Kirkup, the prophet of Bhaal, walked out of the rift. *Blessed Bhaal, savior of worlds has come to cleanse this hive of disgusting good. Glorious evil will flow through here in tides of your blood.*

Colin, Bhaal's orcish champion, walked through, he swung his warhammer at a downed paladin ending his suffering. "Where go?" Colin waited for orders.

*Blessed Bhaal wishes an audience with Tyr. To rip flesh from his corporeal form, to leave him as he was left, damned for eternity. We, his loyal subjects shall be privy to this mission, we shall exterminate the paladins he loves so dear, force Tyr to show, and destroy him.*

"Colin fight."

\*\*\*

The doors to the offices for the Masters of Justice

flew off their hinges and splintered on the boulder of desire. Bhaal walked through the doorway. A paladin ran forwards sword outstretched. Bhaal lifted his finger. It turned into smoke in the shape of a snake and lunged out, piercing the chest of the paladin, killing him instantly.

"Ah, the boulder of desire." Bhaal placed his hand on the boulder.

"Tyr." boomed the boulder. Some of the cultists sniggered.

"I desire his death above everything." Bhaal excused. The cultists sniggered some more before Bhaal stared over forcing them into a nervous silence. Bhaal turned back to the boulder, his arms turned to shadow snakes which wrapped around it lifting it off the pedestal, it cracked and fell to the floor. A trio of gnomes ran out of the shattered pieces, wailing.

Bhaal made for the door to the Grandmasters office.

"Appointment." barked the receptionist, not even looking up.

"You will let me pass or you will die."

"Well, I've never heard a paladin with manners like that. You must be wanting a civilian appointment. I'm afraid the waiting list is substantial due to the cult activities in the area."

"Bhaal does not wait."

"Exactly, that shadowy snake god of death is making all our lives hell. I'm working overtime here and not even getting paid double. Just time and a half, it's a crime I say."

"I am Bhaal."

"Sure you are, love, come back with your army then."

"I have an army, right here."

"Well, they'll need appointments too."

"There will be no appointments!" Bhaal boomed and smashed his fists on the desk. It was only now that the receptionist looked up. She gazed into his menacing red eyes and saw the shadow snakes slithering from shoulder to shoulder. The receptionist waited a moment as she consolidated her thoughts. She looked over to the Grandmaster's door. The archway she had sworn to protect. She peered down at her shattered desk, her mind was made, her thoughts consolidated.

"I was wrong," she spoke staring Bhaal in the eye. "You do have an appointment. With justice!" She grabbed the warhammer she so cherished to use on queue cutters and appointment swappers and launched it at Bhaal. The hammer passed through Bhaal's chest as he went incorporeal and collided with Colin's face who had the most unfortunate positioning. Bhaal returned to his corporeal form and threw the receptionist at the wall. She smashed against it and fell to the floor. From Bhaal's shoulder a shadow snake slithered down and across to her. She tried to get back to her feet but before she could manage the snake was upon her, its teeth at her neck.

Bhaal entered the chamber of the Grandmaster, with Glenn Kirkup and his cultists behind him. "Grandmaster!" he boomed. "Come and face me!"

No reply came from within the chamber. The room was in darkness, with the only light coming from behind Bhaal's forces.

*Bhaal, bringer of death, serpent of misery, destroyer of worlds, nemesis of justice, wishes an audience with Tyr. You will grant his request as your last act on this pitiful plain.*

A shining silver chain shot out of the shadows and wrapped itself around Glenn's neck, whipping him forward and into the ground with a hideous crack. Glenn Kirkup spoke no more.

"Leave this place, Bhaal! Return to your cursed plain or perish!"

"Hiding in the shadows, Grandmaster? Since when has justice feared the light?"

"I'm no fool, Bhall. I know your shadows can't form in the dark."

"Oh, Grandmaster, the darkness is my shadow." Bhaal clenched his fist and the Grandmaster was crushed in an instant, she didn't even have time to scream.

Glenn went to speak but his voice box had been crushed. He knelt hoping Bhaal would bless him by returning his speech. Bhaal looked at him. "Such a disappointment." Bhaal lifted the hat from Glenn's head, returning him to dust.

# PART NINETEEN, RETURN TO THE CITADEL

Barry and Purcee looked up at the ruined Citadel. Plumes of black smoke rose upwards from the shattered building. The smell of death and despair permeated the air.

"So... do you think we were a bit late, then?" said Barry.

"Citadel... destroyed." whimpered Purcee.

"Maybe they're just... renovating?" The left tower of the Citadel crumpled and fell down the mountain. "Uh... I'm sure there was nobody in there..."

Purcee started to march towards the gate.

"Whoa, hey, Purcee! Maybe we shouldn't go in there? The whole Citadel could collapse at any moment."

Purcee turned to look at Barry. "I go," said Purcee. "It is just."

"Just..." echoed Barry. "Fine, okay, we'll do the just thing. I can be just!" Barry hurried after Purcee. They made their way up to the gate. Two guards were stationed there, dressed in ill-fitting paladin armour.

"Paladins, what's the situation here?" shouted Barry.

The smaller guard jumped, startled to see Barry and Purcee. "Situation? There's no situation here."

"Yeah!" said the taller guard. "There's no situations for miles around!"

"Right..." said Barry, looking at the pair of guards suspiciously. "So, can we go in?"

"Um..." The guards looked at each other. "No. No, you can't."

"Why not?"

"Because... of the situation?"

Barry glared at the guards. "Purcee, open the door."

"Oh, you can't do that! The doors locked! That's the situation, you see. Lost the key." Purcee pushed the door. It fell from its hinges and collapsed onto the ground. Inside, the bloodied and burnt bodies of paladins were strewn through the corridor.

"...Oh my goodness!" said the taller guard. "Look at this. There's been... there's been cultists all up in our citadel!"

"How could this have happened?" said the shorter one. "How could we have missed all these cultists? Cultists who are certainly no longer here."

"Wait a minute," said Barry. "It's you two!"

"Us two? Who two?" said the guards.

"You two!" said Barry.

"Well what about you two?"

"Us two?" said Barry.

"Yeah," said the younger monk. "I don't know about you, Terry, but I've never met these two before in this life."

"Mort, you idiot! You just used my name!" said Terry.

"Well you just used my name! We could have played off one of us being called Terry, but Terry and Mort? There's no way that's a coincidence! Now they'll know for sure that we're the monks from the temple in Crystopia!"

"Mort! Stop telling them things!"

The two monks looked over at Barry and Purcee. "Um... Colin!" they shouted. Nothing happened. "Colin...?"

Barry cleared his throat. "Purcee," he said. Purcee picked up the hapless monks and cast them down the mountain. "Thank you, Purcee. Shall we proceed?"

"Purcee."

They headed into the citadel. The smell of burnt flesh lingered in the corridors.

"Where's Clarisse?" Barry asked. "Do you think she's okay?"

"Help." They heard from a room over. "Help me." They ran into the room but there was no one there. "Guys, look down. It's me." Carlos spoke.

"Carlos, why are you on the floor?"

"Silly sword." Purcee contributed.

"Clarisse dropped me as she was dragged away by cultists."

"So she's alive."

"Well, she was alive, but I don't know if she still is."

"Don't you have like a bond with her or something, as she's your paladin and you're her sword? A paladin bond?"

"What... no. That's not how this works."

"It isn't?"

"Do you have a bond with Purcee?"

"What?"

"Cause he's your paladin."

"I'm not a sword, though."

"Oh yeah, I forgot your weren't made with a purpose."

"Do you want us to leave you here?"

"No! There are dead people here…"

Purcee picked up Carlos, "We find Clarisse."

"Where do you think she would be?" Barry asked,

"If it was me I'd hold people in the cells."

"Where are the cells, Purcee?"

"This way." They walked down further into the mountain. Everywhere they went they found the corpses of paladins. Some had been cut to pieces, others horrifically burnt. The worst wounds, though, were those that seemed to have been inflicted by darkness itself. Shadowy tendrils creeped out from puncture wounds, as though they had minds of their own.

"Shadows of Bhaal," said Purcee, solemnly.

"Let's not stick around…" said Barry.

They continued through the winding corridors, encountering no one but the dead. Finally they came to the holding cells. Those too were guarded by the dead, but these dead were standing.

"Carlos…" said Barry. "It's time for you to do your thing."

The skeletons slumped towards Barry, raising crude weapons.

"I don't know if I can kill skeletons…" said Carlos, as the first skeleton swung at Barry, who nimbly dodged it.

"Can't or won't? I need your help here!"

Purcee smashed one of the skeletons to pieces with his axe, but mere moments later the bones reformed and the undead soldier was whole again.

"Well, they are already dead, so I wouldn't be technically killing them, but they're also the living dead, and I'd be stopping them from living..."

More skeletons staggered towards them, Barry did all he could to dodge their attacks, axes and rusty swords swung past him, dangerously close. Purcee swatted away all those he could, but they kept reforming and rejoining the fray. Purcee took a spear to his leg, and he cried out in pain. He grabbed the skeleton that had wounded him and threw it across the room.

"Carlos!" shouted Barry, grabbing the sentient sword and holding it aloft. "You've got to decide here!"

"Okay!" said Carlos. "I'm ethically okay with this!" Carlos started to glow, and a flash of light filled the room. The skeletons stopped their assault, standing motionless around the trio. They turned to dust, their weapons and armour clanged as they hit the ground.

Barry, still holding Carlos in the air, looked at the shimmering dust with awe. "You... you can do that?"

"Yeah... I told you I could take out a whole army of undead, remember?"

"Well, yeah, but, like... maybe you could have done that right away? We almost died."

"You almost died. I would have been fine."

"Carlos!"

"Sorry... Maybe I can kill things that are already

dead, if it means saving my friends."

"Yeah, well… let's not get ahead of ourselves. We're allies."

Purcee pulled the spear out of his leg, he clutched the wound and grimaced.

"Oh, we can help with that! Carlos, do your thing!" said Barry, holding Carlos out to Purcee's wound. But before they could heal Purcee, a black shape emerged from the darkness. Shadowy tendrils wrapped around Purcee, dragging him away.

"Barry!" shouted Purcee.

"Purcee!" screamed Barry, but Purcee was already gone, taken away by the darkness. Barry was left alone with Carlos.

"What do we do now?" Carlos asked.

"Something just," said Barry.

"What?"

"I don't know! Find Clarisse, I guess. Then… Then confront Bhaal."

They walked past empty cells, at the end, dimly lit by moonlight that pierced through the window bars, was Clarisse's cell. They broke open the door.

"Clarisse, are you okay?"

"No, I failed, we failed." Spoke her voice from the shadows.

"What do you mean?"

"I used the red tempered blade on Bhaal and it shattered. He took what was left of the hilt and did this." Clarisse moved towards the moonlight. Where her right eye would have been, now there was nothing.

"Why'd he let you live?"

"There's a ritual Bhaal is preparing for. A ritual to bring Tyr forth into this realm. For the ritual to work, they need to sacrifice a paladin."

"Well, it looks like they've sacrificed plenty of paladins already."

"No, they've killed plenty. But the sacrifice is worse. To corrupt a just paladin into a cultist of Bhaal would infuriate Tyr. It would force his attention onto this realm and bring him into Bhaal's trap."

"We have to face him," Carlos spoke.

"With what, we had a god killing sword and that apparently did nothing." Barry started pacing back and forth. "Geoff told us that if Bhaal wins all sentience will be exterminated. But he said that only Tyr or our weapon could beat him. Why would Geoff lie to us, did he want us to fail?"

"Bhaal is blocking Tyr's presence though, there is no way for us to call on his power, and the weapon didn't work, Barry."

"Why don't we have Purcee, he wouldn't hesitate to face Bhaal, win or lose."

"Where is Purcee?" Clarisse asked.

"He was dragged off by Bhaal's cultists."

"Well then," Clarisse grabbed Carlos from Barry. "I would rather die on the front lines than wait to be exterminated, are you with me?"

"I'd rather not die at all, if that's an option." Barry said.

"Well I can't really die unless I'm thrown back into the fires of Abidurval, but I get the sentiment that you're going for and I agree... with Barry."

"Let's go." Clarisse lead them towards the Offices of the Masters of Justice.

# PART TWENTY, A PALADIN'S END

Purcee was surrounded by Bhaal's serpents. They slithered over his body and bit at his skin. Bhaal laughed at Purcee's torment. "You would make a strong lieutenant, orc, but you chose Tyr's path."

"Tyr true."

"Tyr didn't make you. Your race was created by me, to enslave, and subjugate. I made your race to hold no conscience."

"Purcee care."

"You are nothing more than an abomination. You think you have a soul, you think your sentience gives you control over your destiny, your fate." Bhaal laughed. "You're nothing more than a dog to me."

"Purcee true."

"And you think that will save you?"

"Purcee not need saving."

"You think yourself incorruptible?"

"Yes."

"You're a fool, orc. A disappointment to your race." Bhaal's snakes started to slither into Purcee, via his eyes, ears, nose, and mouth. "Incorruptible." Bhaal laughed. "You are no god, Purcee."

"You know me?"

"A good orc in a realm I set upon a path of destruction. I came here for you Purcee. You are my greatest failure. You forgot your evil instincts. I can feel they do not plague you like they do to all other orcs. Now I'll make sure you experience them, I will control you."

"No." Purcee tried to fight.

"Tyr is a fool, a pitiful god. You devoted yourself to him, hoping it would bring your life value. Know this, Purcee: your life has value. By devoting yourself to Tyr, you have become the perfect tool of his destruction, the weapon I need to at last defeat my enemy."

"No." Purcee whimpered.

"You are no god, Purcee, you can't hope to stop me."

Purcee's eyes went black. Bhaal grinned. Bhaal's cultists stood in a circle around the statue of Tyr. They lifted their hands, a dome curved inwards around the statue. The rock started to crack. An eye could be seen, then stone fell revealing a shield. The dome's red light shimmered in its reflection. There was a breath and then the rest of the stone exploded exposing the form beneath. The dome vaporized the stone into dust as it tried to pass through.

Tyr tried to stand but the dome had him trapped. He looked over at Purcee. "My child." He spoke. "You were chosen." Tyr looked at the ground, rage in his eyes. "They were all my chosen," Tyr's voice reverberated.

"He is an insult, and they were just flesh." Bhaal smiled. "Death comes to all of us. It does not linger today, old god, not for you." The cultists took a step inwards, and then another one. The dome started to push against Tyr's flesh, burning his skin constantly, not allowing it to heal.

"Stop this!" yelled Clarisse, running in with Carlos and Barry.

"Purcee, come over here, get away from Bhaal," Barry pleaded. Purcee turned around, Barry saw the black in his eyes. "What did he do to you?"

Clarisse grabbed Barry by the shoulder. "Nothing good," she said. "Nothing good."

"What do we do?" Barry asked as Purcee moved towards them.

"Purcee smite." Purcee's voice was menacing.

"Purcee, it's me… your friend, Barry."

"Keep him distracted, Barry," Clarisse ordered.

"Me, distract him?" Purcee swung his axe at Barry who dodged out of the way. "Aah! Purcee!"

Clarisse ran past them, searching for a way to free Tyr from his prison. Bhaal blocked her path, his shadow snakes extending outwards to surround her. "Foolish paladin, so eager to face me again? You should have stayed in your cell, or is it a swift death you seek?" The snakes poised, ready to strike.

Clarisse gripped Carlos tightly in her hands. "Fight with me, Carlos. Lend me your strength." The snakes lunged at Clarisse, just as she swung Carlos in a spiral, slicing through them. They fell to the ground and dissolved into nothingness.

Bhaal recoiled in surprise. "What? Impossible! No weapon can harm me!"

"Weapons don't usually talk either. I'm an exception." Carlos gloated.

"What trickery is this?"

"I think this god has forgotten what it's like to be mortal."

"No weapon can harm me," Bhaal said again, in denial.

"I'm no weapon!" Carlos screamed.

"Let's finish this, Carlos!" shouted Clarisse. She lunged forward to deliver the killing blow, but Bhaal turned into a shadow, darting past Carlos and reforming behind Clarisse. Before she could react, Bhaal struck, flinging her across the room and into a wall. Clarisse crumpled to the ground, unmoving. Carlos clanged against the floor.

Meanwhile, Barry was doing all he could to avoid the attacks of his possessed friend. "Purcee! You're not yourself, Bhaal has corrupted you! But you can fight it. I know you can."

"Smite... smite Barry!" said Purcee, swinging his axe down which crashed into the space Barry had been standing only a moment before.

"Think about justice. You like justice."

"Injustice!"

"Oh, Purcee," said Barry. Purcee swung again, slower this time. "You can fight this," Barry pleaded. Purcee hesitated, and then struck out with his shield. Shield touched skin and Barry fell. Purcee looked at his fallen friend as Barry tried to catch his breath. First Purcee's axe dropped, then his shield. Purcee towered over Barry. He grabbed him by the neck and lifted him off the ground. Purcee walked over to Bhaal and dropped Barry at the god's feet.

Tyr looked on from his cage. "Child," said Tyr. "You

are just. Do not fall from the light. Fight back! Your god demands it."

Barry tried to stand but fell to his knees. Bhaal grabbed his throat from behind. "Look into the eyes of your friend, halfing. There is nothing there now, just the abyss. I may bring you back, halfing, once you're gone. I may have you kill for me. Or steal for me. I have a sense you're good at that. Death is a beautiful thing, halfling. It should be emotive, don't you think? Death is a dance where only your partner knows the steps, the timing, the beat." Purcee backhanded Barry. "Do you think you've been in control of your life, halfling? Do you feel you ever had a choice? Do you think any of you get a choice? The orc is the only one in this pitiful realm who ever had a choice, and he chose that." Bhaal pointed at Tyr. Purcee looked at his god, eyes black and empty.

"My child." Tyr spoke. Purcee walked over to Tyr.

"Renounce Tyr." Bhaal ordered.

"Purcee…" Purcee went to speak.

"You have no name, not anymore, orc!" Bhaal screamed.

"Orc, renounce, Tyr." Purcee spoke staring Tyr in the eye. Purcee bent down and picked up Carlos. "What are you doing?" Carlos asked. Purcee returned to Bhaal.

"Do you see that, halfling? All your friends… are your end." Bhaal was strangling Barry now. "I want your last breath to be by my hands, but your death to be at theirs."

"Purcee, please," Barry choked.

Purcee looked Barry in the eye. Black went to white.

Purcee stabbed Carlos through Barry. Barry stared Purcee in the eyes and screamed. Water fell from Purcee's eyes.

Bhaal screamed, the sharp point of Carlos had pierced his chest. From the black depths of his eyes came a glimmer of white. It expanded, clawing its way from his eyes. It leached across his face, and down his body like water tracing down a window. Shadow snakes tried to slither away but the light followed them. It burned through Bhaal like the sun through mist, until there was nothing left. Barry fell forwards. Purcee caught him.

"You stabbed me!" Barry shouted.

"It only way." Purcee pulled Carlos out of Barry's shoulder. Carlos healed the wound behind him.

"You could have stabbed around me!"

"It… only way."

"You could have not used me as an accessory to murder!" Carlos screamed.

"You weren't an accessory to murder, Carlos, you were the instrument."

"That's worse! You can see how that's worse, can't you?"

"Carlos, can't you just be happy that you saved the world from a murder god hellbent on destroying all life?"

"Purcee happy," said Purcee, happily.

In the background Tyr shrugged away the dome that had imprisoned him. Without Bhaal's influence weakening him he had the strength to stand up straight. "Thank you, my child," he said to Purcee. "I knew you were too pure for Bhaal to corrupt you. Too strong." Bhaal's remaining followers scrambled to their feet. They saw that Bhaal was defeated. As Tyr stood and shrugged of the chains, they turned to flee. "I have been far too lenient with this world," said Tyr, raising his hand. "I have allowed chaos and injustice to spread." The cultists screamed, their skin and flesh melting away, the all-consuming fire of justice erupting out of their mouths and eyeballs. "No more. This is my promise to you, child of justice. I shall purge all the wrong-doers in this broken world. All those with ill in their hearts." The cultists fell to the floor, no longer screaming, their lungs burnt away. The flames burnt everything away: their flesh, their bones; their evil hearts and minds. All of it was annihilated by the pure, white fire. The fire of justice. Barry, Carlos, and Purcee watched in horror.

"The beginning," said Tyr, "of the end of this evil world. Once my full power has returned to me, I shall burn them all. Scorch the land and start anew. Only the most righteous shall remain. Those like you, Purcee."

"And Barry," said Purcee.

Tyr looked at Purcee. "And Barry?"

"Barry just too."

"No."

"Yes."

"Barry is a lying, thieving, manipulative little creature."

"Giant small."

"I am very tall for a halfling."

"Barry shall be purged alongside all else who are

unjust."

"Who would be left?" Purcee asked.

"You would be, my child, and those I create for you."

"Who else?"

"Anyone you want me to make."

"Who else spared?"

"No one else."

"I am the only one just?"

"Yes."

"What of the other paladins? What about Clarisse?" said Barry.

"They failed me."

"They died for you."

"They died because they were weak. Now Purcee, say goodbye to this... whelp."

"Purcee?" Barry asked.

"No." Purcee whispered.

"What did you say?" Tyr asked.

"No. You are wrong."

"A god cannot be wrong!"

"This world flawed."

"Yes, Purcee, it is."

"Flawed, good."

"No. This world is like a tree. And you are the apples. But a rot has come, it has infested the tree. It has corrupted the apples and the corruption has spread onwards through their seeds. The tree must be raised, its apples burned so that a new tree can grow in its place. A stronger, better tree, without rot. With holy pure apples. I will grow this new tree, and tend to it-" Before Tyr could finish his sentence Clarisse thrust

Carlos through the back of his head. The white leached through him until, like Bhaal, he was gone.

"Wait, what? What just happened?" Barry exclaimed.

"Why do all the bad guys monologue about apples? That's, like, three times now, if we count the apple troll on the way to Abidurval."

"Ah! I feel sick. Why! Why do you keep disregarding my ethical code when it's convenient to you?" whimpered Carlos.

"I promise Carlos, there are no more gods you'll have to kill," said Clarisse.

"That's cause there's no more gods left!"

"Well…"

"I shouldn't have had to kill any in the first place."

"If there was any other way we would have done it."

"How did I even get in your hand?"

"Yeah, how did he get in your hand?" said Barry.

"Geoff." Purcee spoke.

"Geoff?" Clarisse asked.

"Geoff?" Barry exclaimed. "I thought he wouldn't interfere."

"Balance." Spoke Purcee. "There is balance now." Purcee looked towards the door, it opened and Geoff walked through.

"Who's this guy?" Clarisse asked.

"I am Geoff, Godellfriar of Order."

"Did you do this?" Barry asked.

"I told you I would not interfere."

"But you definitely did interfere."

"I sometimes move things without realising, everyone makes mistakes."

"So you're admitting you interfered?"

"I don't know what you're talking about, halfling. I'm just so happy that there is balance once more and I just knew that I had to see it myself."

"Isn't doing that interfering?"

Geoff moved over and touched Carlos. "To think, the Enchanter took credit for your creation. I pulled you out of the fires. You were made to heal this world."

"Isn't that interfering?"

"No more so than stepping on a blade of grass."

"I feel it kind of is."

"I did not cause these actions to happen, I am merely a spectator."

"But spectators don't physically change the world they are spectating to get an ending that suits them."

"I did not interfere, halfling."

"Yes, yes you did!"

"Now look here, you little shit…"

THE END

Printed in Great Britain
by Amazon